*For Daisy, and for Tom, Sally and Milo*

THE PRINCESS AND THE CASTLE
A JONATHAN CAPE BOOK 0 224 06461 4

Published in Great Britain by Jonathan Cape,
an imprint of Random House Children's Books

This edition published 2004

1 3 5 7 9 10 8 6 4 2

RANDOM HOUSE CHILDREN'S BOOKS
61–63 Uxbridge Road, London W5 5SA
A division of The Random House Group Ltd

RANDOM HOUSE AUSTRALIA (PTY) LTD
20 Alfred Street, Milsons Point, Sydney,
New South Wales 2061, Australia
RANDOM HOUSE NEW ZEALAND LTD
18 Poland Road, Glenfield, Auckland 10, New Zealand
RANDOM HOUSE (PTY) LTD
Endulini, 5A Jubilee Road, Parktown 2193, South Africa

THE RANDOM HOUSE GROUP Limited Reg. No. 954009
www.kidsatrandomhouse.co.uk

A CIP catalogue record for this book is available from the British Library.

Printed and bound in Singapore

# The Princess
## and the
# Castle

Caroline Binch

Jonathan Cape
London

Genevieve hated
the sea.
  She lived right
next to it in a
stone harbourside
house, but kept
away from its
big, cold wetness.

Years ago, she could just about remember, Daddy's fishing boat got lost at sea. He never came home again. Little Jack was born soon after. He cried a lot and Genevieve and her mum cried along with him.

From her bedroom
window, Genevieve
could see the old castle
far away across the bay.

Her favourite game was to be a princess. She imagined her father, the king, lived in the castle waiting for her to come home.

"Princesses don't like beaches," Genevieve would say when her friends called for her on their way down to the shore with their buckets and spades.

Instead, Princess
Genevieve had lots
of adventures riding
her chestnut horse . . .

being kissed awake
by a handsome prince . . .

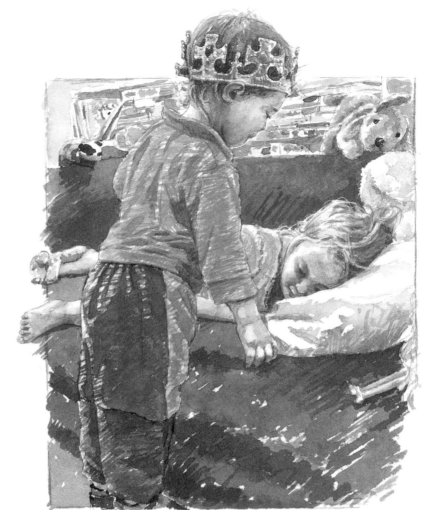

or escaping in the
nick of time from
dragons and monsters.

One sunny morning Genevieve watched a small boat enter the harbour. A tall dark man lowered the red sails.

"Ah, here comes the Red Knight," she told her court.

Some days later Mum introduced
Jack and Genevieve to her new
friend, Cedric.

"Hello, you must be Genevieve,"
said a deep voice. It was the giant,
the Red Knight from the boat.
Genevieve gasped in fright
and fled to
her room.

Mum talked a lot
about Cedric after that,
but Genevieve refused
to meet him again, even
though Mum got upset.
"A scary giant
would try to capture
a small princess," she told
her ladies-in-waiting.
And she hoped he would
not capture Mum.

But there was a
difference in Mum.
She wore pretty new
clothes, smiled and
laughed a lot and
hardly ever got cross.
Genevieve knew that
after she went to bed,
Cedric came to visit
Mum. She became
familiar with the
gentle music from
Cedric's guitar
flowing up the stairs.

Before she knew it, the scary ogre had turned into a big, cuddly and playful bear. They all went out together to the fair and for picnics.

Genevieve was even persuaded down to the harbour shore, riding on Cedric's shoulders.

"Princesses never go in the water," she insisted.

Cedric took them to a lovely cove. "I'm building a castle for the princess," he grinned. They all helped; it was enormous.

"Let's decorate it with shells," said Mum.

Jack and Genevieve played until the sea came right up and tumbled into the moat.

"I'm scared, Mummy," Genevieve squealed.

Even so, she wouldn't
leave Jack alone
on top of the castle
until the sea splashed
at their toes.

They had such fun with Cedric, discovering new beaches. Genevieve became brave enough to paddle up to her knees.

But Cedric and his boat
were another matter.
"No, no, you mustn't
go sailing on the sea,"
she cried, quite
frantic at the thought.
"Mummy, don't let
Cedric go and get lost."
Mum looked worried
too, saying, "Never fear,
my princess, he will be safe."
So when Cedric said one day,
"How would you like to visit the
castle, little princess? We could
sail across the bay," Genevieve was
struck dumb. It was a terrifying idea.
Yet she hated the thought of being
left behind. All her stories were set in
the castle.
      She had to go.

The day of their adventure began.
 "I've got my life-jacket and my
drink," said Genevieve nervously.

Cedric started the noisy engine just to get them
out of the harbour, then he hoisted the sail.
 Genevieve gripped her mum and held tightly to the boat.

After a while,
the gentle rocking
of the boat as it swished
through the sea calmed
Genevieve. She felt safe with
Mum and big strong Cedric.
Scared no more, she stood up, her
princess cloak flapping like the sturdy
red sail that caught the wind and sailed
them across the sparkly blue bay to the castle.

They spent the
afternoon exploring
the nooks and crannies
of the castle.
   Genevieve was surprised
to find no soldiers with swords,
no jewels, no throne and no king!
   But she wasn't disappointed.

They had a
delicious banquet
while looking out
over the bay.
"There's no castle
now," said Mum,
"just our little house
far on the other side."

"I'm a really happy
princess now,"
smiled Genevieve.
"We are in the castle
with our own king,"
and she gave Cedric
a great big giant hug.